Kung Fu Master

Marty Chan

ORCA BOOK PUBLISHERS

Library and Archives Canada Cataloguing in Publication

Title: Kung fu master / Marty Chan.
Names: Chan, Marty, author.
Series: Orca currents.

Description: Series statement: Orca currents

Identifiers: Canadiana (print) 2019006658x |
Canadiana (ebook) 20190066601 | ISBN 9781459822467 (SOFTCOVER) |
ISBN 9781459822474 (PDF) | ISBN 9781459822481 (EPUB)

Classification: LCC PS8555.H39244 K86 2019 | DDC jc813/.54—dc23

Library of Congress Control Number: 2019934037
Simultaneously published in Canada and the United States in 2019

Summary: In this high-interest novel for middle readers, everyone
assumes Jon Wong is a martial arts expert because he's Chinese.

*Orca Book Publishers is committed to reducing the consumption
of nonrenewable resources in the making of our books. We make
every effort to use materials that support a sustainable future.*

Orca Book Publishers gratefully acknowledges the support for its publishing
programs provided by the following agencies: the Government of Canada,
the Canada Council for the Arts and the Province of British Columbia
through the BC Arts Council and the Book Publishing Tax Credit.

Edited by Tanya Trafford
Cover photograph by Stocksy.com/Rob and Julia Campbell
Author photo by Ryan Parker

ORCA BOOK PUBLISHERS
orcabook.com

Printed and bound in Canada.

22 21 20 19 • 4 3 2 1

To Bruce Lee. I tried to be like water,
but I just kept wetting my pants.

Chapter One

Every kid in my grade wants to be my lab partner for one reason and one reason only—I'm Chinese. I don't know who it was, but some jerk started a rumor that Asians are good at math and science. So every time a science project or math homework is due, students desperate to get a good mark suck up to me for help.

Last year Tyler Mason tried to be my best friend around the same time our science projects were due. A peacock with more fashion sense than common sense, Tyler gets by on his perfect smile and smooth confidence. He likes to pretend he doesn't care about appearances. One time he showed up at school with serious bed head. But I could smell the gobs of gel he had used to style his hair into that artful mess.

Tyler became a minor celebrity at our school because of a YouTube video. He filmed himself flipping a half-full water bottle on top of his pet turtle. His post netted 497,876 views. He brags about this number every day. When he approached me, he claimed he could shoot a video of me that would go almost as viral as his had. All I had to do was help him with his science project. And by *help* he meant "do it."

Here's the thing. I'm terrible at math and even worse at science. I can't tell the difference between an acid and a base. The only stars I watch are the ones on Netflix. I would tell you that I'm lousy to the power of ten if I knew what the power of ten meant. When Tyler asked me for help, I turned him down because I knew he'd be worse off with me. But then I learned the hard way that no one turns down Tyler Mason. Ever.

In science today Mrs. Hill rolled out a metal cart loaded with half-full beakers, trays and plastic bottles. She had posted instructions for something called "Elephant's Toothpaste" on the smart board behind her.

"All right, class. Today you're in for a treat. We're going to examine catalyst agents. I think you'll like this experiment."

"Why is it called Elephant's Toothpaste?" I asked.

"You'll see," said Mrs. Hill. "You'll be working in pairs."

I held my breath, hoping she wouldn't leave the choice to us. The last thing I needed was to spend a class trying not to breathe in Tyler's body spray. He uses a lot.

Mrs. Hill scanned the class list. "Tyler, you're with Alanna."

I sighed with relief. Alanna buried her head in her arms on her desk.

Tyler strutted over and plopped himself down on the stool beside Alanna. "You know how many views my YouTube video has now?"

I think I might have heard Alanna scream into her desk.

"Jon, I'm putting you with Megan," Mrs. Hill announced.

Megan Reese is the new girl at school. I don't know much about her other than she is, well, the new girl.

She's only been at St. Thomas More Middle School for a month and she barely talks to anyone. No group has claimed her yet. Not the athletes. Not the gamers. Not the theater kids. She is a loner. But she seems cool.

I looked around. There was Megan, perched on a stool near the back wall. Our gazes locked in a silent battle of wills. I motioned for her to come to my counter, but she shook her head. She pulled her blond hair back in a ponytail and patted the stool beside her. Fine. I shuffled over.

"Hey," I said.

Megan nodded.

"You good at this kind of stuff?" I asked.

She shook her head. "I'm hopeless. I know enough about science to stay away from it."

I chuckled. "I'll beat you to the door."

"On those scrawny legs? I'm surprised they can even hold you up."

"So you like looking at my legs?" I teased.

"I also like looking at photos of autopsies. You remind me of one of them."

I did my best impersonation of a zombie, with my eyes rolled back and tongue hanging out. Megan laughed.

Mrs. Hill rolled the cart forward. "These are some of the things you'll need for the experiment. Come grab a handout and start getting organized."

She reached under the cart and pulled up a huge plastic jug.

"And, if we have enough time, we'll step up the catalyst reactions a few notches with this. But that means you have to focus and get your experiment done fast. No fooling around. Focus on the experiment and not on your phones. And no visiting with each other. That means you, Tyler. In an orderly fashion, go get your equipment, goggles and aprons. *Orderly*!"

Everyone made a beeline for the box of safety goggles, jostling for the most fashionable ones. One girl cheered as she pulled out a pair. Tyler groaned as he held up what looked like the world's ugliest ski goggles.

Mrs. Hill shouted over the din, "No fighting! You get what you get. And remember to wear your safety glasses at all times. Roll up your sleeves. If you have long hair, tie it back. You should know the routine by now. And pay careful attention to the measurements."

As the teacher continued to drone on, I grabbed the handout and scanned the list. Megan read over my shoulder. "We need two beakers."

"I have one already, but we need one more."

"I'll get it."

Megan headed to the equipment cupboard. I tried to decipher the rest of the handout.

"Tyler, the goggles go around your eyes, not your forehead," Mrs. Hill called out.

Tyler grumbled as he slid the goggles over his eyes. I grabbed some dish soap, along with an eyedropper and a couple of bottles of food coloring. Then I headed back to Megan with my tray of equipment. She skimmed the instructions and checked my haul.

"You forgot the hydrogen peroxide and the yeast."

"Okay, I'll be back."

I hustled to the cart with my beaker. Kids were still assembling their materials. Jessie, the girl who loves unicorns and hates everyone else, had hogged the brown bottle of hydrogen peroxide, carefully pouring it into a beaker while the other kids begged her to hurry up. I found the yeast, but the jar was nearly empty. I grabbed it anyway, hoping the few grains left were enough for the experiment.

Mrs. Hill strolled over to where my best friend and his lab partner were already setting out their equipment.

"Nice work, Parmeet," she said. "Don't forget to stir the liquids before you add the yeast."

It would take forever to get the bottle from Jessie. I grabbed the big jug of hydrogen peroxide Mrs. Hill had put on the top of the cart. According to the label, the concentration was 30 percent, but I figured it would still do the trick. I poured some of the liquid into my beaker.

At our station, Megan was holding her head in her hands. She shoved the handout at me and said, "Maybe you can figure this out. It is way too confusing for me."

I stared at the page and then at the smart board. The words were in English, but it seemed like a whole lot of gibberish to me too. But I didn't want to look stupid.

"It says to pour the hydrogen peroxide into a beaker."

Megan held up a narrow tube.

"That's not a beaker," I said. "That's a graduated cylinder."

"Well, that's the only thing that was left in the cupboard."

"Okay. I guess it will have to do."

She placed the tube on top of the plastic tray. I poured the hydrogen peroxide from my beaker into the cylinder. Nothing happened.

"Ooh," Megan said. "Amazing reaction."

"Hold on, hold on. Now we're supposed to add the dish soap and some food coloring."

She added a squirt of red and then some blue. Finally, she poured the dish soap in. We leaned closer and waited. Nothing. I picked up the tube and swirled the liquids.

"Is this the way it's supposed to work?" I asked.

"The yeast. We forgot to add the yeast."

"This was all that was left," I said, holding up the jar. I tried to sprinkle the yeast into the tube, but most of it landed on the counter.

"Maybe we could use something else," said Megan. She scanned the sheet. I peeked over her shoulder.

Tyler slid in beside Megan. "Ours is a dud too," he said, elbows on the table. "What's happening here, Megs?"

Megan shrugged. "I think we're doing something wrong."

"No way. Not with Jon Wong. He's 'Mr. Science,'" said Tyler. He always thinks putting air quotes around words is hilarious.

My face grew warm. "We're supposed to work in partners," I said. "Not trios."

"Yeah, well, Alanna is busy. Thought I'd see if one of you wanted to trade your safety glasses out for these cool specs." He tapped the goggles back up on his forehead. "What do you say, Megs?"

Megan narrowed her gaze at him. "*Megan*. My name is Megan."

"Whatever."

"Hey, Jon," said Megan, trying her best to ignore Tyler. "Maybe we can find a YouTube video and see what we're missing."

"Good idea," I said.

Tyler fished his phone out of his pocket. "What? Mr. Science didn't think of that first?"

Megan grabbed Tyler's phone and tapped the screen a few times. Then she set his phone on the tray so we could all see the scientist pouring liquid into a tube.

"Yeah, we added the dish soap. And the food coloring. Oh, wait. What's that?" I asked.

"Potassium iodide," Megan said, squinting at the screen where the scientist was holding up a bottle and droning on. "Maybe we could use that instead of the yeast."

"I didn't see any of that stuff on the cart," said Tyler.

"Tyler, get back to your own station," called out Mrs. Hill. "And put your goggles on!"

"Why?" whined Tyler. "I hate these things. They fog up, and they leave red marks on my face."

"Come here, Tyler. Right now."

Tyler sighed, pulled the goggles over his eyes and shambled over to Mrs. Hill.

"Maybe there's some potassium iodide in the cupboard," I said.

"Cool. I'll get it," Megan said, slipping off her stool.

I watched Mrs. Hill reading Tyler the riot act. He had bothered me enough times that I enjoyed it when he got busted.

Megan came back with a little tub. "The video didn't say how much potassium iodide to use. What do you think? A tablespoon?"

"Sure."

Megan measured out the white crystals and added them to the cylinder. The liquid instantly turned to foam and began climbing up the tube.

"Whoa!" we both said at the same time.

The multicolored foam shot straight up to the ceiling before raining down on top of our tray and Tyler's smartphone.

Chaos broke out as kids started screaming. I wiped some of the foam off my safety glasses.

Mrs. Hill rushed over. "What did you guys do? Wait. Did you use the hydrogen peroxide in the jug?"

"Sorry, Mrs. Hill. I didn't know it was going to do this."

"That much is obvious, Jon," she said, scanning the smoking pile of foam now covering our table. "But it still shouldn't have reacted like this. Did you use anything else not on the list?"

"Um…" I said. "I might have added some…potassium iodide?" I decided not to bring Megan into it.

"*What*?"

"Sorry," I mumbled.

Tyler plunged his hand into the foam. "My phone! Look at what you did to my phone!" He looked like he was about to drop me.

Mrs. Hill stepped between us. "That's enough, Tyler. It's just foam. You can wipe it off."

"The stuff is on my screen. If you wrecked my phone, Wongie, you're going to pay."

"Tyler, get back to your station. Jon, clean up this mess. Megan, can you help? I have to call maintenance."

"Yes, Mrs. Hill," Megan said. She went to grab some paper towels from the dispenser by the classroom door. When she came back to our station she whispered, "Thank you."

"No problem," I said.

Well, one problem. Tyler. He was glaring at me from across the room. He made a slicing motion across his throat.

Chapter Two

Rumors about the lab accident spread quickly. By the end of the day, the kids had coined a nickname for me—"the mad scientist." No one even mentioned Megan.

By my locker, Parmeet clapped his hand on my shoulder. With his spiky black hair with blue tips and his rapid shifts from one thing to another,

Par reminded me of Sonic, a character in the video game Dad used to try to make me play. "There he is. The one and only mad scientist. Way to go, Jon. Everyone's talking about how you wrecked Tyler's phone."

"I saw him using it at lunch. I think it's okay."

Par chuckled. "The kids are saying you were trying to get out of science class."

"What? No. It was a total accident."

"So? What happened?"

I sighed. "It's no big deal. We couldn't figure out the instructions, so Megan pulled up a YouTube clip. Only it wasn't the same experiment."

"I'll say. Why did you take the blame for it?"

To be honest, I wasn't sure why. "I thought maybe people would stop thinking I'm good at science."

"Yeah, but now they think you're a mad scientist. You should have let Megan take the fall."

"Megan's new. I didn't think she should have something like this stick to her."

"People will forget," Par said.

"Sure, says the boy who peed his pants."

"Come on, Jon. That was in fifth grade. And I'm telling you, the water fountain overshot. That's all."

"Yeah, yeah, yeah. It was the *water fountain* that overshot. Right onto your crotch."

"Hey, you want to check out a movie this Friday?" asked Parmeet.

"Changing the subject? Smooth, Par. Smooth."

"There's a new Jee Ling flick. *Feet of Fury.*"

"Who's Jee Ling?"

"Only the best martial arts action star to come out of Hong Kong since Bruce Lee. Everyone's talking about his sick moves on screen. Parkour plus wushu plus, plus, plus, plus. He's the real deal."

"What's the movie about?"

"International bad guys do bad things and give Jee Ling an excuse to kick butt. C'mon, man, what else do you need to know? You in or not?"

"Sure, sure. I guess."

"Meet you at the theater at six thirty. And don't be late. I want good seats."

"Okay, okay. I'll be there."

The rest of the week was a rough ride. The story of the lab disaster grew with every retelling. By Friday the kids thought I had been trying to build a bomb, and it was only Mrs. Hill's quick thinking that had saved everyone. Tyler continued to harp on me about his broken phone even though I could see him texting from it all through language arts class. I needed a break from the rumors and from Tyler.

Par was waiting for me outside the theater. He tapped his watch.

"You're late, Jon."

I beamed at him and held up my phone. "Yeah, but I've already booked our seats. Just have to pick up the tickets."

"Oh man, you are the best. Thank you, thank you, thank you."

"You buy the popcorn and drinks. And no cheaping out. I want extra butter on my popcorn, you hear?"

"Okay, okay," he said.

I scanned my phone under the ticket dispenser and waited for the machine to spit out our tickets. Then I joined Par in the lineup for the concession stand. At the far end, behind the counter, I spotted someone familiar.

I elbowed my pal. "Par, Par. Look who's behind the counter. Megan."

"Oh yeah. Looks like she's got her hands full."

"What?"

"Check out who she has to work with."

Beside Megan, Tyler scooped popcorn into a bag. He was joking around with Megan, a giant smile oozing across his impossibly clear face. I swear that guy must have sandblasted the zits off and slathered himself in plaster. No one has skin that smooth. Ever. Megan did not look pleased.

"I think I'll skip the popcorn," I said.

"What? Come on, Jon. I owe you."

"No, I'm good."

"Oh, I get it. You have a crush on Megan. You *like* like her," teased Par.

My face felt suddenly hot. "What? Are you nine? No I don't."

Par laughed. "Yeah, you sound convincing. You take the blame for her and now you are too shy to order popcorn from her? Yeah, dude, you are totally crushing on her."

I didn't want to tell Par that the real reason was because of Tyler. Ever since the lab incident, I had been waiting for him to come at me hard.

Par nudged me ahead. I stepped back, but he hooked his arm around me and guided me toward the counter. Megan beamed at me. I returned her smile and mumbled hello.

"Hey, Jon. What movie are you going to see?"

"*Feet of Fury*," Par said. "Hi. I'm Parmeet. You can call me Par."

"Hi, Par. You guys on a date?"

He shook his head. "No. Why would you think that?"

She nodded at Par's arm around my waist. He quickly let go.

"It's totally cool that you're dating."

Par stammered, "No, you don't get it. I was just...well, it's complicated..." He trailed off.

I cracked a grin. "We're trying to make his boyfriend jealous."

She smiled. "Well, I think that's sweet."

"Thank you," I said.

Tyler slithered up beside Megan, holding a bag of popcorn. "What's sweeter than you?"

She rolled her eyes.

Tyler turned and fixed a death glare on me. "Oh hey, if it isn't the mad scientist and his sidekick, Igor."

I gritted my teeth. "Can we get some popcorn?"

"Two bags," Par cut in.

"And two sodas."

Tyler hid behind the bag of popcorn. "Oh no! Don't sell him any Mentos and Coke. He might blow up the movie theater and destroy everyone's phones."

"I *didn't* wreck your phone," I said.

"It's been acting up ever since the lab," he said. "I want a replacement, so you'd better start saving, Wongie. I'm going to get a lawyer if you don't cough up the cash or a new phone."

Just then Megan turned and knocked the popcorn out of Tyler's hand. I couldn't be sure, because it all happened so fast, but it almost looked like she meant for it to happen. Kernels fell to the counter and floor.

"Oops, clumsy me." She turned and winked at us.

Beside us, the woman who had been waiting for the popcorn that was now spilled across the counter glared at Tyler. She growled, "I'm going to miss the trailers, kid."

"Sorry, sorry. I'll fill this up," said Tyler quickly.

"I want a new bag. And extra butter."

Par paid Megan for our snacks. We hurried away even though I kind of wanted to stick around and watch Tyler get yelled at some more. I glanced back at Megan. She waved at me.

"I think she knocked the popcorn out of Tyler's hands on purpose," I said to Parmeet.

Par shook his head. "Nah, it was an accident. A happy one."

"Yeah, I suppose. No one could move that fast."

"Jee Ling could. *Hiya!*"

I shook my head at Par as we entered the theater.

Chapter Three

Par and I weren't the only ones who saw *Feet of Fury*. At school on Monday everyone was buzzing about Jee Ling's acrobatic martial arts moves. Par tried to recreate a fight scene in which Jee Ling had taken out four guys while keeping his hands behind his back. In the movie, the scene played out like a ballet. In the school parking lot, Par looked more like a penguin trying to kick toilet paper off his foot.

"*Hiya! Yee-aah!*" Par shouted. "Oh, you want some? Come and get it."

I laughed as my friend waddled in front of me.

"Come on, Jon. Spar with me."

"I don't know the first thing about kung fu."

"Tiger claw. Drunken monkey stance. Crane about to take flight." He mimed various animal poses, making his own unique sound effects as he whipped his arms and legs into place. "Teach me, sifu. I am a sapling in your shadow."

I laughed. "Okay, you must be like the willow in the wind. Never break, but always bend." I crouched and pulled my pants up before motioning Par to come at me.

"Beak of the eagle about to snatch the early worm," he screamed as he charged ahead.

I lifted a hand to ward off his blow and then pretended to strike him in the stomach. Par reacted as if he had been hit with a sledgehammer and staggered back, clutching his ribs. Then he waved his arms in giant circles while swiveling his head to and fro.

"Par, what are you doing?"

"I saw Jee Ling do it in the movie."

"Not even close. It was more like this." I snaked my arms and crossed one foot in front of the other. I finished with a flourish of stabs in the air. My hands were cobras striking invisible opponents.

Slow claps filled the air, stopping me in the middle of my routine. My face flushed. A crowd of teens surrounded us.

Par punched his fist into his hand and bowed. "Sifu, thank you for the lesson."

"What are you doing?" I mumbled out of the side of my mouth.

"You are a great teacher, Jon. I am humbled in the presence of a kung fu master."

One of the kids called out, "Show us another move."

The others nodded. "Yeah. We want to see more."

I backed away. I was about to tell everyone that I was no kung fu master, but I stopped when I spotted Tyler at the back of the crowd. His flawless face was scrunched up as he watched the other kids jostling to get closer to me.

"Back up, everyone," Par said, stepping in front of me like a bouncer. "Don't crowd my sifu."

"What is a sifu?" a girl asked.

"Sifu is what you call a kung fu master," Par said. "And this is my sifu. A great teacher of the martial arts."

"Can he teach me something?" asked a gangly kid named Benton. He looked like a living scarecrow with his stick arms and shaggy hair.

"I'm sorry," I said. "I can't teach you anything."

"Why not?" Tyler asked, shoving his way to the front.

"Well, uh, it's because kung fu isn't meant to be for fun. It's a serious form of martial arts."

Tyler crossed his arms over his chest. "Oh really? Well, I for one don't think you're any kind of kung fu master. Show us something other than waving your arms in the air. I want to see you take someone down."

I shook my head. "Fighting on school property and getting expelled? No thanks. I'm not dumb."

He clucked. "Chicken."

Par stepped in. "Listen. Kung fu isn't some kind of children's game.

It's serious. Jon's people have learned it over the centuries as a kind of self-defense, but it is so much more now. It's a way of being."

"Looks like he's ducking out of a challenge," Tyler said to Derrick, one of his pals.

Derrick screwed up his freckled face and said, "That guy's all talk and no action."

"Talk? More like *bwock, bwock, bwock, bwock*," Tyler clucked.

I wasn't going to bite, even though I seriously wanted to punch him in the mouth. "A true kung fu master doesn't need to prove himself."

Tyler flapped his arms and clucked.

The other kids laughed. I hated that they could turn so quickly from admiring disciples to nasty bullies.

"Come on, Foot of Fury, show us what you've got," said Tyler.

I glared at him.

"Guess he's all talk and no action. Stick to solving math problems, Jon."

I gritted my teeth and ground my foot into the pavement, lowering my body into what I thought was a fighting stance. "Okay, you want to see something? Watch this."

A hush fell over the crowd as I motioned for Par to step in front of me. He nodded. I locked my gaze on his eyes, willing a silent message. I hoped he'd received it, but I couldn't tell for sure.

"Attack me," I ordered.

He charged at me with his fist raised over his head. I followed the punch and stepped to the side, letting it fly right past my nose. He had slowed his punch enough for me to react.

"Again!" I barked.

He took another slow swing at me, which I blocked with my arm. Then I slammed both hands against his chest, stopping just before I made any real contact. He stumbled and landed on the ground.

A hush fell over the crowd.

Par raised his hands in surrender. "I yield, sifu."

The kids cheered and rushed closer. Their voices filled the air.

"Amazing!"

"Fantastic!"

"Do it again!"

I lifted my hand for silence. "That is enough for today."

"Lucky shot," Tyler said, sniffing the air.

"Maybe you should teach us," Benton said.

"I do not teach those who are not ready."

The kids moved closer, begging to be my students.

"Please? Just teach us one move," a girl said.

Benton said, "I'm ready to learn."

Tyler piped in. "If you were a real kung fu master, then you'd be willing to share your secrets."

Let it go, will you? What a jerk.

I glanced at Par for help, but he shrugged, still sitting on the ground.

I bit my lower lip for a second before giving my answer. "I will consider it. Let me think on it," I said.

The morning bell rang, and we all filed into the building. Tyler glanced back at me, that smarmy smile on his face. I helped Par to his feet.

"What did I get myself into?" I asked.

"I don't know, man, but you'd better hope the kids forget about kung fu lessons, and soon."

"Or else what?"

"Or else Tyler's going to ride you for the rest of the year."

I nodded.

Par was right. Tyler was bent on revenge, and the only way out of it was to prove him wrong. The only problem was, I had no idea how to do kung fu.

Chapter Four

That night Par and I got together at his house. His parents have a ginormous TV. It fills one wall of the living room, with a snake's nest of cables running to two different video game consoles. Par sat cross-legged on the throw rug, a keyboard in his lap, and his fingers resting on the keys.

"What are we looking for?" he asked.

"Any video on how to do kung fu," I said. I planted myself a few feet away from the massive screen. The thin carpet and my ratty sweatpants gave little comfort against the hardwood floor underneath.

The screen lit up with a screenshot gallery of kung fu masters. I scanned the images of men and women in kung fu outfits posing in battle stances. The images seemed more like screen grabs of movies than instructional videos.

"Next page," I said.

"What about the one at the bottom?" Par asked. He pointed at the screenshot of a kid in a white karate outfit, standing on one leg with arms outstretched like a crane.

"That's *The Karate Kid*," I said.

"Original or reboot?"

"Doesn't matter," I replied. "It's karate. We want kung fu."

"What's the difference?"

"Karate is from Japan. Kung fu is from China."

"I know that. I meant what's the difference if you learn the moves from a movie or a real instructor? No one's going to call you on it. *You're* the expert."

"Yes, but I'm not about to tell people how to paint a fence or wax a car. They might catch on."

"Fine. I'll keep looking."

Another set of images appeared on the screen. The top three were movie images, but the fourth one looked like it had promise. I pointed. "That one, Par."

The image expanded to fill the entire screen. A man with long hair, wearing a plain white T-shirt and black pants, adjusted a red sash around his waist. Judging by its quality, I figured this video had to be at least twenty years old. The man looked into the camera, punched his fist into the palm of his other hand and bowed to us.

"Good day. I'm Sifu Bob. Today I'm going to introduce you to the incredible world of the martial arts."

Par butt-skidded across the carpet to get closer to the TV. The smile on his face was almost brighter than the screen.

"I can't wait for this. I'm so going to be a kung fu expert."

"I need something I can use to fool the kids at school."

"Jon, you're halfway there. You're Chinese."

"What's that have to do with anything?"

"You're a natural at this."

I shook my head. "I'm a klutz when it comes to any kind of sports. Remember the floor-hockey incident in elementary school?"

He laughed. "Yeah. Shoot the ball, not the stick. You know, you *could* come clean and just admit that you don't know any kung fu."

"And give Tyler more ammunition? No way. The last thing I need is another reason for him to make fun of me."

"Okay. Let's see if we can shut him up."

We turned our attention to the video. Sifu Bob crouched like he was sitting on an invisible stool. He took a few breaths and centered himself, with his hands resting on his hips.

"The horse stance is the most basic stance, but it is one you'll need to master. Watch again how I get into position."

Sifu Bob straightened up and put his feet together. Par stood and imitated the actions, beckoning me to join him. I reluctantly got to my feet.

"With your heels together, swivel your toes away from each other as far as you can comfortably. Now swivel your heels out. Then your toes. Now straighten out your feet so they are parallel to each other. That should place them about the right distance apart."

I felt like I was learning dance steps with the most boring instructor in the world. Beside me, Par had gotten himself into position and was starting to crouch. I tried to imitate Sifu Bob.

"Lower yourself until your knees are at a ninety-degree angle," said Sifu Bob. "Keep your back straight. Pretend you are trying to sit in an invisible chair."

"More like a toilet and I'm about to fall in," I said.

Par laughed and fell on his butt. He sprang back up immediately and tried again. I maintained my pose. The backs of my legs burned as I tried to hold the position.

"You will know you are doing it right if you can put a stick in your lap and it does not roll off," said Sifu Bob.

"You have a stick handy, Par?"

"No, but I don't think you've quite got the angle right. Try crouching lower."

I bent my legs as far as I could go. Suddenly I heard a rip. *Did I tear a muscle?* Then I felt a draft between my legs. Par broke out laughing. I straightened up and looked behind me.

"What? What's the matter?"

"You ripped your sweats, dude."

"Aw, nuts."

"Yeah, I can almost see your junk."

I pulled my shirt out of my pants to try to cover the rip. "Okay, kung fu lesson number one. Wear looser pants."

On the television, Sifu Bob continued, "Do this for a few minutes every day, trying to maintain a straight back and a ninety-degree angle for your knees. This is your base stance. From this position you'll be able to center yourself for the series of moves that I will teach in the next videos. Keep your form. That is the most important thing."

"Par, I think this might be a good start. I could kill at least ten minutes with this."

"Yeah, but people are going to want to learn some real moves. Not how to squat."

"Skip ahead. See if this guy teaches any kicks or punches."

Par headed to the keyboard and tapped. On the screen, more images of Sifu Bob appeared. One of the videos was entitled "Tiger Claw." Another was labeled "Praying Mantis."

"Try the tiger claw," I said.

"On it."

The video clip played. "Now we are going to try the tiger claw. Assume the horse stance. Hold your hands out with fingers raised in the air and palm perpendicular to the ground. Now curl your fingers inward as if you were trying to crush a tennis ball. Keep the tension in your fingers, but relax your wrist.

Now strike forward with one hand while pulling back the other. The opposing movements will give you power for your tiger-claw strike."

Par and I practiced the tiger-claw punch for several minutes, until the video ended.

"Not bad, kung fu master," Par said.

"I say we put it into action. We could have the kids face off against each other. Turn and face me. Horse stance."

"Yes, sifu." Par crouched in front of me.

"Tiger-claw strike."

His hand snaked out and smacked me in the chest. I staggered back. "Ow. What was that for?"

"Sorry. You were standing too close."

I rubbed my chest. "Okay, I'll have to learn to give instructions from a distance."

We watched a few more Sifu Bob videos, plus a training scene from Par's favorite kung fu movie—*Snake in the Eagle's Shadow*.

"You'll get a kick out of this. This was Jackie Chan's first movie ever."

A young Jackie Chan with a full head of hair danced around several wooden poles planted in a line. Behind him, a gray-haired sifu held a basket. Jackie snaked his hand up each pole to grab an egg and toss it in the basket.

"Cool," I said. "Now that's what I call a training session."

Then the scene switched to the old man holding a rice bowl and daring Jackie to knock it out of his hands. Jackie lunged, jumped, twisted, punched and kicked, but the old man with the gray beard easily stepped out of the way. Sometimes he even tossed the bowl on top of his head while Jackie flopped around on the ground, always missing his target.

By the end of the night, I figured I had pieced together enough to fake my way through a lesson. Par sparred with me, eager to try out the moves we'd seen in the videos, adding a few of the moves from the Jackie Chan movie. He looked like a mime trapped in a giant plastic bag who really needed to pee.

"Okay, Par, settle down. Let's see if we can run through a drill."

"Ready, Sifu Jon."

"I like the sound of that. Yes, let's use it. What should I call you?"

"Something Zen-like. *Disciple* sounds too much like a cult. And if you start calling me an animal, it'll sound like you're teaching a stuffie."

"How about just Par?"

"Yeah. Okay."

"Par, horse stance," I barked.

He crouched with hands at his side.

"Tiger-claw punches. One! Two!"

"*Hiya!*" said Par.

"Now, monkey charges lotus!" I commanded.

Par skittered forward.

"Kick!"

"Ya!!"

Par's foot shot straight out and stopped, but his shoe kept flying. Everything went into slow motion as we watched his stinky missile arc across the room. It was headed for an antique lamp on the end table. Par and I tried to intercept it, but the shoe struck the lampshade.

Smash! The lamp shattered on the floor.

"Nooo!" shouted Par.

Par's dad called from the kitchen. "What was that?"

I checked an invisible watch on my wrist. "Wow, look at the time. I have to go. Bye!"

I sprinted out of the house, but not fast enough to miss hearing Par's dad yell, "Parmeet! Look at what you did!"

"I can explain, Dad," I heard Par reply in a shaky voice.

I didn't catch any more. I was running down the street. Sifu Jon's number two kung fu lesson? Practice far away from breakables.

Chapter Five

Par couldn't join me for my training session on Sunday. His dad had grounded him for breaking the lamp. So I was on my own to go over the drills and routines for my "lesson." I went down to the local rec center.

I had borrowed my dad's sweats. They were about two sizes too big for me. That was a good thing though.

No chance of any embarrassing rips with these baggy pants. I practiced the horse stance in front of the mirror, carefully swiveling my feet out.

After a few minutes I noticed Megan in the reflection. She was over at the other end of the gym. She was working some bicep curls. Her sleeveless T-shirt showed off her muscular arms. She must have sensed me watching, because she turned around. I resumed my horse stance, pretending I was focused on my own reflection.

Megan grunted and pumped a few more curls before setting the weights on the floor and wiping off her bench. She walked toward me.

"Nice horse stance," she said.

"What? I mean, oh, yeah. Thanks."

"So the rumors are true. You do know kung fu."

I straightened up. "What are people saying?"

"That you're some kind of martial arts expert. I think I overheard someone say you trained with Jee Ling over the summer. And somebody else said you're related to Jackie Chan."

"Yeah, well, you know what rumors can be like."

"So you're *not* related to Jackie Chan?"

"Actually, I'm his second cousin."

"What? Really? That's so awesome!"

I laughed. "No, I'm just kidding. The only thing we have in common is that we're both Chinese. That's it."

"Oh. Still, it's cool to meet someone else who is into martial arts."

"So you're into kung fu?"

She punched her fist into her palm and bowed. "Been training since I was nine. My brother was taking kung fu lessons, and Mom only had time to drive us to one activity a week.

She gave me a choice. I could do my homework while he was doing his kung fu, or I could join in. Now he's the one sitting on the sidelines doing *his* homework."

"Wow, since you were nine. You must be pretty good. What belt do you have?"

She cocked her head to the side. "You in kung fu or karate? Belts are for karate."

"Oh, right. Yeah, I knew that," I said quickly. "I meant *sash*. I'm so used to people asking me what belt I am that sometimes it's easier to just say *belt*."

"I hear you. I'm blue. You?"

"I'm black and blue," I joked. "Tough drills."

Megan looked at me a little strangely. "So where do you train?"

"Oh, you wouldn't know my studio."

"Is it Gingwu? Wing Chun? I know all the kung fu studios around here."

I inched away from Megan, eyeing the exit. If she pressed much more, she'd figure out that I was lying.

"Actually, I'm in between studios right now," I said. "Anyway, I should probably get back to my workout." That was my lame attempt to change the subject.

"Well, if you want, we could train together."

Megan did a flurry of air punches in front of me, turning her hands into knife blades as she twisted her body and moved toward the mirror.

I nodded. "Not bad. Not bad at all. I'll have to think about it."

"Come on, Jon. I'd like to have someone at my level to do forms with. The only class that I can get to has no one of my age and level. I have to do forms with eight-year-olds."

"Maybe."

"Okay. Well, I'm always up for a training session. You text me, or I'll text you." She unclipped her phone from her armband and swiped a thumb across the screen. "What's your number?"

"Uh...well...I'm not..."

"You between phones too?"

I laughed. "No, no." I gave her my number. I had no intention of training with Megan. But I had to get her off my back.

After she had keyed in my number, Megan glanced up. "You know, everyone is pretty excited that you're going to show off your moves at school next week."

"Yeah, well, I thought it might be a way to get people excited about coming to my sifu's studio."

"I thought you said that you were between studios."

"Right, right. Well, to be honest, it's kind of embarrassing." Oh man, this was hard! "The reason I'm between studios is because mine isn't getting enough students to stay open all the time.

My sifu is struggling. I thought this might be a way to get him new students."

"Wow. That's honorable," said Megan. She looked impressed. "My studio," she continued, "is super busy. My sifu complains he barely has time to clean up after all the little kids who come to his classes. I wish we had some older students. Hey, maybe I could visit your studio and train with you there. I know you're probably more skilled than I am, but I can try to keep up."

Time to check my invisible watch. "Oh man. I'm running late. My mom's supposed to pick me up in five minutes. I have to go. See you at school?"

I hustled out of the gym, not daring to look back. Sifu Jon's number three lesson? When you're in the presence of a real kung fu expert, say little and get out as fast as you can.

Chapter Six

At school I wanted to avoid everyone, especially the kids looking for kung fu lessons. Even though I had rehearsed my routines, I had lost my nerve after my run-in with Megan. She would see through me the minute I started teaching. I couldn't stand the idea of being called out as a fake in front of Tyler.

I skulked into the school before anyone could spot me and hid in the back of the library. I slid between two bookcases and leaned against the wall. I wanted to spend the rest of the day here, away from Tyler and eager disciples. I pulled a sketchbook and pencil from my backpack and began to draw a masked warrior in a kung fu pose.

Drawing comes naturally to me. I love the way simple shapes connect together to make a picture. Three ovals can make a leg, and a bean shape can form a body. Sometimes when I look at objects and people, I search for the different shapes within them. Right now I was staring at the rectangular book that was hiding my face from anyone who might walk by.

The first bell rang. I didn't budge from my spot until the second bell. I peered through the shelves at the hallway. Nearly empty. I got up and headed for the door. I wanted to be the last one in class so I didn't have to talk to anyone about kung fu. I trudged toward my homeroom like a guy being sent to the principal's office.

All eyes turned to me as I entered the classroom. I nodded at Par and slipped into the desk behind Megan.

Mr. Lee took attendance. "Anyone see Tyler today?"

No one responded. Maybe today was going to be okay. Maybe I could get away without having to do any martial arts. My faint hope was crushed when Tyler sauntered in.

"Sorry, Mr. Lee. The principal needed some help carrying in some stuff from her car. I was happy to lend her a hand. I guess it took longer than I thought."

"That's fine, Tyler. Have a seat."

The bell rang for the start of first class. About half of the kids sprang up from their desks and headed to the door. The rest of us stayed in our seats. Our first class was language arts with Mr. Lee.

Megan turned around. "Hey, Jon. So when are you going to teach the kung fu lessons?"

Darn it. Did she *have* to be so keen? "I'm not sure. Maybe at lunch."

"Everyone's itching to see what you can do."

Par moved to the desk beside me. "Yeah, I've been talking it up. We should get a great crowd."

I swallowed hard and took a quick peek at Tyler. A group of his followers had gathered around him. He faked a karate chop in the air and whispered something to his friends. They burst out laughing.

I turned to Par and Megan. "Maybe let's put it off till the end of the day."

"Sure, sure. You're the sifu," Par said.

"Okay, class," Mr. Lee said. "Settle in your seats. Come on, sleepyheads. Move it. Hustle. The longer you take to start, the longer I keep you after the bell."

The students shuffled to their desks and sat down.

"We're going to pick up where we left off on Friday. In *Life of Pi*, what do you think the tiger represents? Anyone?"

Tough way to start a day, Mr. Lee. No way anyone was going to volunteer an answer. I knew from firsthand experience that the person who tried to answer the first question was the teacher's go-to for the rest of the class.

"You all read the book. Come on, there's a tiger in the boat. Is it real? Or is it not?"

Megan slowly raised her hand. "I think it's real. Well, as real as a rumor."

"Interesting. Do you want to expand on that, Megan?"

"Well, we can't really trust the narrator. He's getting the story secondhand from a guy who claimed it was true. So it's kind of like gossip. The tiger is real to the person who is telling it."

"Ah, yes, Megan. Nice point. So is there any way of figuring out who, if anyone, added the tiger?"

"I don't know. It's like that old game, 'broken telephone.' I played it once at my old elementary school. When you pass the message on from one person to another, it changes. It doesn't matter who changes it. It changes, and it's up to the person hearing the message to decide if it's real or not."

"Not bad, Megan. It's nice to see that someone here has been paying attention. Now, who would like to talk about the allegorical references in the book?"

Suddenly everyone became really interested in the tops of their desks. I'd never seen an entire class drop their heads that fast.

"Anyone?" Mr. Lee asked. No one looked up. "Well, I guess no one wants to answer because they'd rather write a whole essay on the allegory in *Life of Pi*."

Groans filled the air.

"Do we have to?" Par whined.

Mr. Lee smiled. "No, my friend, you can go sit in the corner and play with stuffies and take a nap if this class is too hard for you."

"I *can*?"

Everyone laughed.

"No, Parmeet. You have to do the work like everyone else."

"Oh."

"Grab a laptop from the cart and get started."

For the rest of the class, I stared at the blank screen and tried to will an answer to appear. No luck. I tapped a few keys, trying to start a sentence.

Life of Pi *is a book by a Canadian author named Yann Martel. It is a good book. And it has allegory in it.*

Ugh. Terrible. I tried to start over. Mercifully, the bell rang for next class. I slammed my laptop shut and joined the line of kids stowing the laptops in the charging cart.

Tyler lingered near the back. He taunted me. "Beep, beep. Loser alert. Loser alert. Beep, beep."

I ignored him and headed out. For the rest of the day I avoided Tyler and the lackeys who hung around him. I needed to find a way to get out of this mess. I thought about faking food poisoning, but I didn't have the nerve to stick my finger down my throat to force myself to puke. Instead I stared at the clock and counted down the minutes to my doom.

Chapter Seven

After last class I met up with Par at his locker.

"Well? Are you ready, Sifu Jon?"

I bit my lip. "It's now or never, I guess. Where are my disciples?"

Par pointed to the end of the hallway. A few kids were gathered there. I took a breath, straightened up and walked toward them. As soon as they saw me approaching, they grabbed each other and started whispering. I noticed Tyler and three of his buddies were among the group. Ugh. But no sign of Megan. At least one thing was going my way.

I stopped in front of the kids, punched my fist into my palm and bowed to the group. They looked at one another, unsure of what to do.

"Bow to the sifu," barked Par as he turned to me and bowed.

Most of the kids awkwardly copied his move. Tyler and his pals just watched.

"Step outside the school, and I will introduce you to the ancient art of kung fu," I said. I was laying it on thick. "A student must be committed, dedicated, patient and, most of all, respectful of the master."

Par nodded. "Yes, sifu."

The others nodded in agreement. I glanced back. Tyler and his goons followed but said nothing. I was sure the heckling would start soon enough. I led the kids to the other side of the fence so that we were no longer on school property. The last thing I wanted to do was get in trouble with the principal.

We entered a nearby park and found an empty spot on the grass, away from a group of old men playing chess on stone tables. A few joggers ran down the path near us, but no one was paying any attention to me. I stepped in front of the kids and put my hands on my hips.

"You will not become kung fu experts overnight. Learning martial arts takes years of attention and focus. You must commit to daily practice or else you will never improve. We will start with the basic stance."

Everyone shifted from one foot to the other. Tyler whispered something to his pals, and they laughed. I ignored them as I stepped into the horse stance, using the heel-toe swivel method I had picked up from Sifu Bob's video.

"This is the horse stance," I announced. "This is the first thing every student needs to master. Watch."

I repeated the heel-toe method. At the back of the crowd, Tyler and his buddies began to hum the "Chicken Dance" song as I spread my legs.

Par growled at them. "This is not the time for games."

I ignored them. "Do as I do. Heels together. Point your toes in opposite directions. Swing your heels past your toes. And then move your toes out."

Tyler clapped four times, as if he were punctuating the "Chicken Dance." I continued to ignore him and focused on the kids attempting the horse stance. Some were into it. Others were taking their cues from Tyler. I was losing half of my group. I had to win them back.

"With the horse stance, you have a stable base. Par, come at me."

He nodded and struck a pose while I squatted into the horse stance. Today I was wearing jeans, so I was sure there would be no ripping. Par aimed for my head as we had rehearsed. I punched once from my position and stopped short of his body. He staggered back, clutching his chest, and fell to the ground. He should have got an Oscar for his performance.

Everyone clapped.

"As I said, the horse stance gives you power."

Tyler called out, "You did that earlier. Show us something new."

I shook my head. "It is important that we start with the basics. Now, get into position."

Everyone did the heel-toe thing and settled into their squats. Tyler sniffed the air and waved at his friends to leave.

Two followed him. The other boy squatted into the horse stance along with everyone else.

I started by running the kids through an introductory routine where they would punch from the horse stance and then try to step forward a few steps and kick. Before we knew it, half an hour had passed. To indicate we were done for the day, I punched my fist into my palm and bowed. This time the kids didn't need Par to remind them to return the bow.

"We want to learn more, Sifu Jon," Benton said. "Will you give another lesson?"

I shook my head. "I don't have the time."

"Please," said Alanna.

"Yeah. Just one more lesson," begged another disciple.

Par stepped in front of me and waved his hands for silence. I could count on my friend to bring this nonsense to an end.

"Okay, if you want to learn, we'll hold an advanced workshop this weekend, but you're going to have to pay. Twenty bucks per person. Cash in advance."

"What are you doing?" I muttered to him.

"Trust me," he muttered back. "Sifu Jon doesn't come cheap," he continued for all to hear, "but he's willing to give you a break for this once-in-a-lifetime lesson."

Everyone was nodding and chatting excitedly as they walked away.

"Are you *nuts*, Par?" I said when they were out of earshot.

"Easy money, man! If we get five students, we can make a hundred bucks. Split seventy for me. Thirty for you."

"Why do you get more? Not that I'm saying I'm going to do this."

"Think of it as my service fee. Relax. We'll watch a few more videos and fake our way through."

"No," I said. "There's no way we can fake that much. They're going to expect much more. We have to call it off."

"No way. Not with all the money we could make. Tell you what. Let's scope out a kung fu studio and see how the pros do it. I might be able to sneak a phone in and film some of the action so we can use it."

"I don't know…" Par was always getting me into stuff like this.

"Have I ever let you down?"

"Well, there was the time—"

"*Lately*. Have I let you down lately?" Par said.

Before I could answer, he turned and started walking home. I followed. Sifu Jon's number four lesson? Don't let Par do the talking.

Chapter Eight

Par and I scoured the internet for local
kung fu studios. Par found the website
for the Dragon Academy of Kung Fu,
which was advertising an open house.
We decided to go check it out and see if
we could pick up any pointers.

Once we found the place, we huddled
at the back with a group of moms and

dads watching the young kids practice drills in front of a large mirror. At the front of the class, a Chinese woman in a white T-shirt and black pants paced back and forth, correcting postures and occasionally nodding and smiling.

At the far end of the studio there was a shrine with a large portrait of an old bearded guy above it on the wall. The original sifu, I guessed. There were candles underneath the image, and a bowl of oranges. The rest of the wall was filled with racks of kung fu swords and spears. On the other end, above a mirror, a row of Chinese lion heads, the kind you'd wear in a parade, sat on a long wooden shelf.

Par leaned over to me. "I'm going to record some of this so we can study the footage later. Cover me." He slipped his phone out of his pocket and stood behind me, aiming the camera at the students doing their drills.

I crossed my arms and kept an eye out for anyone who might notice us, but most parents were more interested in watching their kids. A few moms stared at their phones. A couple of kids, bored siblings probably, played games on their tablets. One kid was mining for gold in his nose. I shuddered at the thought of what he might find up there.

"Jon?" A girl's voice behind me.

I stiffened and nudged Par to put away his phone. I turned around and came face-to-face with Megan, now decked out in her training gear. A dragon logo stared at me from her white T-shirt, and a blue sash was tied around her waist.

"I just came out of the changeroom. I thought it was you guys. You're here to train? Or are you looking to steal some of the students for your studio?"

I smiled and shook my head. "We're checking things out. I'm keeping a low profile. I don't want my sifu to know I'm shopping around."

"I can give you a tour. Or if you want, you can join in. It's an open house today, so anyone can go on the mat."

"I'm in my street clothes. Maybe next time."

"Come on, Jon. Everyone on the mat is in street clothes. This will give you a chance to meet my sifu and decide if he can take you to the next level."

"Some other time," I said.

"Or maybe you could become one of our teachers."

Par elbowed me. "We should go, Jon."

Megan blocked our path. "What's your rush?"

"We have to get to our training," I mumbled.

"Does that involve looking at the video you just shot in my studio?"

"I don't know what you're talking about," Par said.

"I saw what you were doing." Megan looked from me to Par and back again.

I shook my head. "We weren't doing anything."

"Then let me see what's on that phone."

Par started to put his phone in his pocket, but Megan's hand shot out and grabbed his wrist. She was as fast as a cobra.

"Ow!" Par said, his eyes wide. "That hurts. Let go!"

"Not until you tell me what you guys are really up to."

"Scoping out the competition," Par whined. "We wanted to see what makes your studio so popular."

She twisted his wrist.

"Ow! Ow!"

"Try again. It's pretty clear that Jon is no kung fu master."

"What? Of course I am." I'm not sure why I wanted to make things worse.

"I didn't want to correct you at the gym, but your horse stance was weak. And I spotted you training the kids in the park. I don't know what you were teaching them, but it wasn't kung fu."

I bit my bottom lip.

"I could always ask Tyler," Megan continued. "Didn't I see him there?"

I waved my hands at her. "No, no. Don't talk to him."

"Then come clean. What's your game?"

I sighed. "It's just that Tyler is such a jerk about picking on me. I wanted to shut him up. When the kids saw us horsing around the other day and thought I was a kung fu expert, well, I couldn't say no. Not with Tyler watching."

"Oh yeah, he can be a bit much," Megan said. "Still, that's no reason to fake being a martial arts expert. People can get hurt, you know. And if you prop them up with false confidence, they might pick a fight and really get hurt."

"Sorry," I said. "I wasn't thinking."

"No, you weren't. But why are you here?"

I mumbled, "We thought we could learn a few moves. The kids wanted me to teach them some more."

"You think you can pick up a lifetime of learning in one session?"

"We didn't mean to disrespect what you do," Par said.

"Yeah, we really didn't," I added. "I just didn't know how to get out of the jam I was in. I was desperate."

"Well, there's one thing I will say," Megan said, her frown softening.

"You can't let Tyler get away with mistreating you. He picks on other people because he can't do anything himself. He's nothing, and his opinion has about the same weight."

"Easy for you to say. You're not a target."

She cocked her head to one side. "I work with him at the theater. You think that's any fun?"

"Oh right. I forgot."

"Megan, can I have my hand back?" Par interrupted. "I'll delete the video."

Megan let go, and Par immediately tapped the screen. "Done," he said. "Sorry," he added.

"We promise we won't bother you again," I said. "Come on, Par."

"What are you guys going to do now?"

I shrugged. "Maybe I'll move to a new school."

"Witness protection?" Par suggested. "When Tyler learns Jon was faking it, he's never going to stop riding him."

"That's my problem," I said, "not yours, Megan. Sorry again for bothering you."

Par and I made our way out of the studio. When we got to the far end, I stopped and bowed to the picture of the sifu. I'd seen the other students doing it when they entered and left the training area. Outside, Par and I walked toward the bus stop.

"Okay, I have an idea, Jon," said Par. "We could tell everyone that your sifu found out you were trying to train the kids and told you it was forbidden. And you have to honor your teacher, right?"

"You think Tyler would fall for that?" I asked.

"You never know. What else are you going to do?"

"I'll figure out something. Maybe I'll get lucky and a meteor will hit the school tonight."

"Or how about just Tyler?" said Par with a grin.

I smiled back. "Dare to dream, Par. Dare to dream."

Just then my phone buzzed. I pulled it out of my pocket. It was a text from Megan.

I want to help.

Chapter Nine

That weekend I turned our basement into my kung fu temple. With Megan's help, we were going ahead with the training workshop. Megan borrowed a couple of spears and swords from her studio to display on the concrete wall under the tiny basement window. I wanted to recreate the shrine I had seen in her studio. I covered a stack of boxes with a bedsheet and set a bowl of oranges on top, along with a framed photo of my grandfather. I would pretend he was the original sifu of my temple. The plan would work as long as the kids didn't notice Grandpa was posing in front of the Disneyland castle.

Megan wore her kung fu outfit. I put on the silk jacket Mom made me wear on Chinese New Year's, plus the dress pants I'd worn to my uncle's funeral. To complete the outfit, I put on a pair of Dad's old slippers.

As Par welcomed the students into my kung fu temple, I stood ramrod straight with my hands clasped behind my back. Beside me, Megan stood at the ready, like my second in command. Par bowed to me as he entered. The seven kids behind him did the same and then lined up along the wall.

"Welcome to the Temple of Doom," I said. What can I say? I am a fan of the old Indiana Jones movies.

The kids looked at each other.

"Sifu Doom's knowledge has been passed down over the generations." I swept my hand toward the photo of Grandpa and then stepped in front of it before the kids could get a good look.

A few "oohs" echoed in the basement.

"What you learn here within these walls must stay within these walls. The martial arts you will learn do *not* grant you permission to pick a fight. In fact, the fight you will have is the one within you. You must conquer your inner fears and doubts. Only when you master yourself will you become a kung fu master."

The kids nodded. They looked so serious! Par stood behind them and gave me a thumbs-up. He flashed a fistful of bills, then jammed them in his pocket and joined the line.

I nodded at Par, stepped back and waved my hand at Megan. "This is my number one student. She will teach you some of the basics of kung fu. You will listen to her as you would listen to me. Is that understood?"

The kids nodded again.

"I *said*, is that understood?"

"Yes, Sifu Jon."

"Then let us begin. Megan?"

Megan bowed to me, then turned to the kids and unleashed a series of punches in the air, followed by a flurry of kicks. She finished with a spinning back kick. She jumped so high, I thought she could fly. The snap of her leg sounded like the crack of a whip. I had to look away so the kids wouldn't see the shock and awe on my face. I had to pretend this was a normal training session, but I wanted to break out in applause.

"Don't worry," said Megan, now standing in front of the kids. Their mouths were all hanging open. "Sifu Jon doesn't expect you to learn that on your first day. Maybe on the second one."

Everyone laughed.

"Okay! Show me your horse stance," continued Megan. I nodded knowingly as she spoke, doing my best to play the part of the wise master, proud of what my student had learned. "Legs apart. Bend your knees. Ninety degrees. Back straight. Let's go!"

For the next fifteen minutes, Megan worked on helping everyone properly position themselves into the horse stance. I walked among the kids, correcting their postures, using the tips Megan had fed me before the session. "Bend lower. Back straight. Your feet are too close together."

Every time I gave advice, the kids beamed. Megan was obviously doing all the heavy lifting, but my occasional comments seemed to have a real impact.

"Nice straight back."

"Thank you, sifu," Alanna said, her braces gleaming in the light.

"Your feet should be parallel to each other."

"Yes, sifu!" Benton shouted.

"How's this, sifu?" asked a kid named Jagmeet. Sweat poured down his face. He was clearly determined to hold this position until he got it exactly right.

"Excellent, Jagmeet. Great form," I added. As if I had a clue.

I had to admit I liked the attention. At one point I even walked over to Megan and commented on her form. "Your knees must be at ninety degrees. Back straight."

She raised an eyebrow but nodded and said, "Thank you, sifu."

Par started dishing out the compliments. "Great job, Alanna. Ooh, I like your stance, Benton. Imagine how great you'd be if you took more lessons."

"No talking, Par," I barked. I knew he was angling to get more money, but I was having none of it.

"Sorry, sifu."

"Focus on your training," I said. "Master your own discipline. Do not let yourself be distracted. True kung fu masters have complete control over their bodies, including their tongues."

Par tilted his head at me but said nothing. I continued to drone on about the importance of kung fu and controlling the mind, stealing lines from all the kung fu movies I had ever seen. I even threw in some of the stuff I remembered from the Sifu Bob videos.

I kept giving pointers to all the students, even Megan. She gritted her teeth but did as I said. When the session was over, I asked everyone to show me what they had learned.

"Horse stance," I ordered.

They snapped to it and crouched.

"Tiger-claw punches. One, two!"

They punched the air in front of them with their claws.

"Front kick."

In unison my students took a step forward and kicked the air. Some feet were higher than others. One girl's shoe came flying at me. Instinctively, I raised my hand to protect myself, and by some miracle, I caught it.

A collective "wow" filled the room.

"That was amazing!" Alanna said. "Teach us one more move, Sifu."

"Yeah!" Benton added. "I want to learn that trick."

I shook my head. "That's enough for one day."

"Please," a chorus of voices begged.

"I'm not sure if I have the time," Megan said, but no one was paying attention to her.

"We might have a special offer for more lessons," said Par.

I glared at him.

"I want to learn that spinning kick you taught Megan," added Jagmeet.

The way the kids looked at me with wide eyes and broad grins, I couldn't resist milking the moment. "Of course, hers is very good, but mine is higher, faster and deadlier. It took me years to master that particular kick, and Megan is only starting to learn. If she puts in the years I have, she might just become half as good as me. Just as you must all put in the work to be even a tenth as good as me."

The kids all nodded. Megan said nothing.

I put my hands up dramatically. "Now you must leave my temple so I can get on with my meditation. Thank you for coming."

"Aw. Please. Just a little longer," Benton begged.

"The master needs his rest," Par said.

I shook my head. "I will not be resting. I will be meditating. There is a difference."

"Can we watch?" Alanna asked.

"Well, it would cost you," Par said.

"No. This is my time," I said quickly. "Thank you for coming. You can leave. My assistants, Megan and Par, will show you out."

My friends stiffened.

I clapped my hands. "Well? Do I have to tell you again? Hurry up. Go, go."

Megan and Par glanced at each other and then began leading the kids up the stairs. I stood in the middle of the room, posing for the kids as they left. Once I was alone, I started to clean up the temple.

Megan came back down, but Par did not.

"I think that went pretty well, don't you?" I said to her.

Megan collected her weapons and stomped back up the stairs without saying a word.

"Megan? Megan! What's the matter?" I called.

She didn't answer. All I heard was the door to the basement slamming shut.

Chapter Ten

For the rest of the weekend I tried to get hold of Par and Megan, but neither would answer my texts or calls. I wanted to relive the experience of the temple with my friends. I wanted to tell them how awesome it had felt to be a sifu and have all the kids looking at me with respect. I finally gave up.

I rewatched the training sequence from *Snake in the Eagle's Shadow* and tried to imitate the moves that Jackie Chan's sifu did with the rice bowl. I twisted and turned my body, trying to keep my rice bowl from hitting the floor. I was glad I was using a plastic bowl. Otherwise, I would have been sweeping up broken glass all day.

At school on Monday I tried to find my friends. I saw Par in the schoolyard briefly, but he hustled away in the opposite direction.

"Par, Par. Wait up!" I cried.

I chased after him, but going around the corner I nearly slammed into Tyler and his pals. They were huddled around a phone, watching a video.

"And now look at how many views I have," Tyler said.

"Cool," one of the boys said. But it sounded more like a yawn.

I tried to skirt around them. I was nearly in the clear when Tyler spotted me. He spread his arms and held back his friends.

"Be careful, guys," he warned. "He might drop-kick us all the way to China."

"Tyler, your act is getting old fast," I said.

"Oh, I thought it was *your* act that was all wet. No, wait, that's what you did to my phone."

The guy just couldn't let it go. "It was *foam*. Your phone is fine."

"It's been buggy ever since you sprayed that goop all over it."

"I highly doubt it."

"What? You think I'm lying?"

I shook my head. "Whatever."

"You know, Jon," Tyler said, flashing his smile at his pals, "I heard you didn't even teach your 'workshop' on the weekend." He used his famous air quotes again. "I heard you let Megan do all the work."

I shrugged. "She's my best student. Everything Megan knows she learned from me."

Tyler laughed. "Here's the thing, Wongie. I don't think that's how it is." *Uh-oh.* "I think *she's* the one who knows kung fu, and you're nothing."

"Think what you want, Tyler, but I know what I know." I started to inch away from the gang, but kids were gathering around us. Why is it that when two people face off against each other, everyone has to come and watch?

"I'm not going to fight you, Tyler, if that's what you're aiming for."

"Chicken."

I clenched my fists but didn't say a thing.

"If you're a real expert, it will be a quick match," said Tyler. "Tell you what. I'm going to be at the park after school. Maybe you show up. Maybe you don't. If you do, we might have some fun. If you don't, we'll all know exactly what kind of kung fu master you are."

"Big talk from a guy surrounded by his friends," I said lamely.

The other kids shifted, restless to see some action. A few muttered, "Fight, fight, fight."

"These guys? They'll just watch. Right, guys?"

His pals laughed and nodded.

"Well, Jon? What do you say?"

I glared at Tyler, then glanced at the crowd now standing around us, eager to see me in action. I don't know why I let this jerk get under my skin. I just knew that I wanted him to shut up for once in his life. I scanned the crowd for any sign of Megan or Par. Neither were around. I was on my own.

"Okay," I said. "After school."

A collective "oooh" erupted from the kids.

Tyler beamed. "I'll be there, and I'll be taking bets on whether or not you show up."

His friends clapped his back and covered their mouths. I think I heard them mutter, "Burn."

"You'll lose that bet," I said, but I wasn't so sure about it.

Tyler walked away with his friends. The crowd broke up, but I could hear everyone chattering about the fight after school. I had to find Megan and Par. Sifu Jon's number five lesson? Always have backup. Always.

At lunchtime I finally found Megan and Par. They were sitting against the lockers in the hallway, and they both spotted me at the same time. They got up and started walking away from me.

"No, wait!" I cried out. "I need to talk to you guys."

They walked even faster down the hall. I sprinted to catch up to them.

"What do you want?" Par asked.

"I need your help."

Megan scowled at me. "Well, that's strange. You seemed pretty capable of handling yourself this weekend. I don't think you need us at all. We're just your *assistants*."

"What are you so mad about? I didn't do anything."

Par's nostrils flared. "Seriously? What about the way you treated us on the weekend? Like we were your servants."

Megan agreed. "And you took all the credit for the work I did in the training session."

"Yeah, well, I was supposed to be the sifu!"

Par shook his head. "In front of the students. Not in front of us."

"I don't see what the problem is," I said. "I was just playing a part."

Megan glared at me. "Yeah, well, it looked like you were really into it."

"Guys, forget about that. Tyler just challenged me to a fight. I have to get out of it. You have to help me, Megan. I *need* you."

"Oh, so *now* you think you need me. Convenient."

"I don't want to get in a fight, but I don't want to back down either. What do you think I should do?"

"Whatever you want," said Megan. "Come on, Par. I think the air is a little too stuffy around here."

"Yeah, it's thick like smug."

"You mean smog?" Megan asked.

"No, I don't," said Par.

Then they walked away. I couldn't believe my friends were abandoning me in my hour of need.

Chapter Eleven

My last class of the day was culinary arts. I had signed up because I thought I'd get free food. I hadn't thought about the fact that I'd have to cook too. Turns out I am a terrible chef.

I scraped a pile of burned eggs out of my frying pan. It was supposed to be an omelet, but instead it had become a science experiment.

My teacher smiled bravely. "Nice try, Jon," he said. "Did you put oil in the pan first?"

"Oil? Oh, right. I knew I forgot something."

"Please try to remember next time. We're running out of usable frying pans."

He strolled to the next station. I resumed excavating the burned bits from my pan. I was taking my time cleaning up. I wished I had a time machine so I could go back and undo agreeing to fight Tyler. Actually, I wished I could travel all the way back to when people had first asked if I knew kung fu. I would tell them that not every Chinese person is a kung fu master or science whiz.

I dumped the frying pan into a sink of dishwater to soak. As I started putting away the eggs, I considered not even going to the park. But Tyler would never let me live that down. For half a second, cradling an egg in my hand, I wondered if I could start a food fight and get a detention. I looked around for a target.

I stopped and stared at the egg. I had a better idea. It was a long shot, but what other options did I have? I slipped the egg into my shirt pocket and headed out of the class.

At the park, Tyler and his buddies were waiting for me. So was what looked like the rest of the school. I hated that the promise of a fight attracted so much attention. Why couldn't I get the same number of people out for the slam poetry night I had hosted the month before?

I searched the crowd for Par and Megan, but there were too many faces. I slowly walked toward the group.

Tyler straightened up when he saw me approaching him. "Whoa, it's 'Kung Fu Master'! I thought you weren't going to show up at all. Looks like I owe

Derrick ten bucks. You know I'm good for it, right, Derrick?"

"Probably not," said Derrick, pulling his cap over his eyes. "You still haven't paid me back for the past seven lunches I bought for you."

"Add it to my tab. So, bigshot, you ready to do this?"

I scanned the crowd again. In the middle I spotted Megan and Par. I smiled at them, but they didn't smile back.

"You looking for help? I don't think Megan's going to bail you out on this one, are you?"

Megan crossed her arms and said nothing.

"Tyler, I came here to tell you that I will not fight you," I announced loudly enough for everyone to hear.

"I knew it! Coward," Tyler sneered.

I shook my head. "You said you want me to prove that I know kung fu. A true master doesn't need to fight to prove his skill. A sifu has the confidence to know that when he must fight, he will do so. And he has the humility to know that when others help him, he will return the favor and show them the respect they deserve."

"What are you talking about, loser?" Tyler asked.

"I am sorry," I said, looking right at Par and Megan before turning back to Tyler, "but I will not fight you today or any day."

"You hear that, everyone? He's too chicken to fight. I win." Tyler danced around, pretending to be a boxer celebrating a victory.

"But I will show you that you are no master either," I said.

Tyler stopped in mid-dance. "Say what, little man?"

I pulled the egg out of my pocket. "A sifu can show their skill without ever throwing a punch or a kick," I said.

"What's that egg have to do with it?"

"If you can snatch this egg from my hand, I will admit that I'm no expert and that you are the better of the two of us."

Tyler laughed. "You're going to wear that egg, loser."

"If that's what you feel you must do. I deserve no less for not treating kung fu and those who believe in it with the respect they deserve." I turned to Megan, locking gazes with her.

Suddenly Tyler's hand shot out and grabbed the egg. He held it up, and everyone gasped.

"That was too easy," he said, tossing the egg from hand to hand.

"I wasn't ready," I protested.

"Too bad. Now you're going to get what's coming to you," said Tyler, moving in on me. "You're going to pay for what you did to my phone."

"I didn't wreck your phone, Tyler." I was feeling remarkably calm, considering I was about to get pounded. I channeled my inner sifu.

"You know you did. Admit it," he said.

"Do as you must."

Tyler grinned at his buddies and then raised the egg over his head. He started to bring it down on my head.

I tensed, waiting for the yolk to spread across my forehead, but someone tapped the back of my knee, causing my leg to buckle. Then a shoulder nudged my body to one side.

Tyler staggered forward when my head wasn't where it was supposed to be.

Beside me, Megan whispered, "Let your body relax, and I'll take care of the rest."

"What?"

She slipped behind me as Tyler roared and charged at us. I raised my hands to protect my face. Megan grabbed my right shoulder and pulled as she tapped the back of my knee, causing me to bend farther backward as Tyler's hand swished past my face.

"Stand up!" Megan hissed.

I straightened up and turned to confront a red-faced Tyler. He charged at me again. Megan swept my left leg out as she hooked her arms under my armpits and pulled me to the right. Tyler tripped on my outstretched leg and landed flat on the grass.

He pushed up from the ground, his face covered in egg yolk. Everyone laughed as he wiped egg and grass from his face. "What are you laughing at?" he shouted. "Shut up! This isn't funny!"

"That's what I call egg fu!" Benton said.

Tyler rose to his knees and pointed at me. "You all saw it. He beat me up. You're witnesses to this assault."

"Are you kidding, Tyler?" Par cried out from the crowd. "All we saw was you fumble around and hit yourself with an egg."

Everyone laughed again.

"Shut up! I did not!"

"Had enough, Tyler?" I asked.

He climbed to his feet. For a second I thought he was going to charge again, but then he swung at me with a wild sucker punch. Megan's hand pushed hard on my shoulder again, forcing me to duck the blow. A loud smack filled the air. Then a collective gasp.

Tyler backed away, his eyes wide. "I'm sorry. I didn't mean to. It wasn't my fault."

I turned around. Megan was holding a hand to her cheek. She looked shocked.

Everyone was silent.

Tyler tried to explain. "I didn't mean to hit her. I was aiming for Jon. I'm sorry, Megan. I really am."

Megan stared at Tyler hard. "So, are you still going to tell the principal that

Jon beat you up? Because I think my story will be better."

He put his hands together. "Please, don't. I'm sorry. I didn't mean to do it."

Megan held up a hand to silence the crowd. "Tell you what, Tyler. You walk away, and we can forget this ever happened. But if you try any more crap like this, I have witnesses who will back me up."

"I swear. I'm done with Jon. Promise. I'm sorry, I'm so sorry."

"Get out of here before I change my mind."

He nodded and slunk away. Everyone watched him go. No one followed, not even Derrick or his other pals.

I turned to Megan. "Are you okay?"

She cracked a smile as she pulled her hand away from her cheek. There was no sign of injury. But I noticed that her forearm was a bit red. "Blocking is as important as punching," she whispered.

Then she put a finger to her lips. "Shh. Our secret."

The kids gathered around us.

"You should tell the principal," Alanna said. "Tyler shouldn't be allowed to get away with it."

Megan shook her head. "It's not worth it. And I think I'll be okay. I need to get some ice on my face."

Par crossed his arms. "From now on, anyone who hangs out with that jerk is on my list."

Derrick stared down at his feet. The other guys also avoided meeting Par's glare. I guessed that Tyler was going to be quite lonely for the next little while.

"You two were awesome," Benton said. "I've never seen anyone move like that before. What kind of kung fu was that?"

I glanced at Megan. "You'll have to ask her. She's the sifu."

She beamed at me as the kids crowded around her to ask questions. I was happy to be left on the sidelines. A few feet away from me, Par tried to get closer to Megan.

"Give her some space, people. If you want to learn what she does, it will cost you."

I smiled. Par never changed. He glanced over at me and winked. Then he returned to trying to make a buck off the moment. Sifu Jon's final lesson? Kung fu is not for everyone. Especially me.

Chapter Twelve

The kids started to leave the park. I figured Par's hard sales pitch had scared them off. Megan, Par and I strolled together to the main road.

"For someone who likes to dish it out, Tyler sure can't take it," Par said.

"Yeah, most bullies are like that," Megan said.

"Hey, guys, I'm sorry for acting the way I did," I said. "I wanted Tyler off my back so bad, and when the kids started looking up to me, well, I guess it went to my head."

"I'll say." Par started miming his own head getting bigger like a balloon.

Megan laughed. "No, it's more like this." Her balloon head expanded until it popped.

"Yeah, I deserve it. I'm really sorry. It sucked so much when you weren't talking to me."

Par grinned. "Megan wanted you to stew for a bit. We never thought you would show up at the park."

"What choice did I have? Tyler wasn't going to stop."

"Yeah, he was going to egg you on," said Megan.

Par and I groaned.

"Weak, Megan, weak," I said. "You should probably stick to kung fu."

"Where did you get the idea for the egg anyway?" asked Megan.

Par raised his hand. "I know, I know. *The Snake in the Eagle's Shadow*. First Jackie Chan movie. Best one ever. Except didn't his sifu use a rice bowl?"

I nodded. "I thought the egg would be more dramatic. Plus, it was easier to sneak an egg out of class."

"Well, it was impressive until he took the egg away from you," Megan said.

"No, *you* were impressive!" said Par. "How did you make Jon move like that? Do they teach that at the studio?"

Megan shook her head. "You're not the only ones who watch kung fu movies."

We laughed. "Thanks for bailing me out," I said.

Megan stopped. "Oh, that's sweet. You think I was doing it to be nice."

"You weren't?" I was confused.

She shook her head. "Nope. Now you owe me one, Jon."

"You are absolutely right," I said. "I sure do. And after what you did for me, I'm willing to do anything for you."

"Good. Keep up that positive attitude," Megan replied. "You're going to need it."

Par grinned. "Wait a minute. So what exactly do you have planned for my pal?"

"For both of you."

"Me?" asked Par. "What do I owe you for?"

"For trying to make a buck off kung fu. Come with me."

We followed Megan to her kung fu studio. She bowed to her sifu on the mat, and he wandered over.

"Megan, good to see you," he said. "You're here to train?"

She shook her head. "No, Sifu. I remembered you said you were looking for more help around the studio. These guys are willing to volunteer."

"Excellent. I know just the thing for them."

An hour later Par and I sat in the viewing area, polishing the kung fu sword blades with rags. My hands reeked.

Megan came over to check on our progress.

"How many weapons do you guys have?" I asked.

"My hands look like my grandma's," Par whined.

Megan smiled. "Good."

"Are we done yet?" Par asked.

She shook her head. "We're just getting started. After this, the sifu said he wants you to clean the lion heads."

She waved a hand at the giant Chinese lion heads up on the shelf. Their wide eyes stared at us.

"You'll have to comb the tangles out of the manes and spritz the inside of the heads with a special spray made from essential oils. They can get a little funky after a while."

"Please tell me this is some kind of secret training drill like in *The Karate Kid*," Par said. "Wax on, wax off."

Megan laughed. "Keep thinking that if it helps you work harder. And, guys, I want to see my face in the reflection of those blades. If I don't, then you're going to have to start over."

I sighed and returned to my polishing. I held up the blade to check out my reflection. My short-lived career as a kung fu master was over. But I didn't mind one bit.

Acknowledgments

Thanks to Nicole Schatz, Nicole Lafreniere, Nick Riemann, Megan Tsang, Sifu Bill Gee, Sifu Brendan Lee, Stephen Tsang, Dustin Archibald, Wei Wong and Michelle Chan.

Marty Chan is an award-winning author of dozens of books for kids and plays for adults. He tours schools and libraries across Canada, using storytelling, stage magic and improv to ignite a passion for reading in kids. He lives in Edmonton with his wife, Michelle.